Me and My Puppy

By Terri Diffenderfer
Pictures by Paul Frame

Copyright © 1990 McClanahan Book Company, Inc. All rights reserved.
Published by McClanahan Book Company, Inc.
23 West 26th Street, New York, NY 10010
Printed in the United States of America
ISBN 1-878624-41-5

Every time Mommy and I went into town we passed the pet shop. And every time we stopped to look at the puppies in the window.

"Can I have a puppy—PLEASE?" I always asked. And Mommy always said, "Sorry, we're just looking."

Yorkshire Terrier

Dalmatian

Basset Hound

Dachshund

St. Bernard

But this time we went INSIDE the pet shop!
There were big puppies and little puppies. There
were black puppies and white puppies.

Boxer

Blood Hound

German Shepherd

Shar Pei

Cocker Spaniel

There were puppies with straight hair and puppies with curly hair, puppies with pointy ears and puppies with floppy ears.

Now I wanted a puppy more than ever! So I asked, "PLEASE can I have a puppy, Mommy?" And this time Mommy said YES!

Right then I knew just the puppy I wanted. It wasn't the biggest. It wasn't the littlest. It wasn't even the prettiest or the most handsome.

It was the one that stood up right in front of me, poked her nose through the cage, and wagged her tail. It was the FRIENDLIEST!

At last I had my puppy. And when Mommy asked what I was going to name her, I said, "FRIENDLY!"

Before Mommy and I left the store, we bought
Friendly all the things she needed. We bought:
a red dish for food,
a blue dish for water,
puppy food and puppy biscuits,
a collar and a leash,
two toys,
and a basket to sleep in.

When I walked out of the pet shop with
Friendly tucked under my arms, I knew I had to
be the happiest boy alive.

That night, Friendly curled up in her new bed, all cozy and snug, and she fell fast asleep. And I knew she was happy, too.

I decided I would show Friendly all around the
house the very next day. But she found ME first!
Off with the covers . . .

. . . and up onto the bed she went. Friendly
jumped all over me and licked my face.

But I wasn't the only thing my puppy found.
She found Daddy's socks, Daddy's hat, and one of
Daddy's shoes.
Daddy didn't like that very much.

Then she found Mommy's pearls, Mommy's
favorite sweater, and one of Mommy's plants!
Mommy didn't like that very much.

One time we left Friendly in the house by herself for just a little while. She found a roll of toilet paper!

And when Friendly found the garbage can and knocked it over, I didn't like it very much at all! (I had to clean up the mess.)

Mommy and Daddy said that every puppy must learn to behave. So I had a talk with Friendly.

SIT!

STAY!

GOOD PUPPY!

Then I started to teach her. It was hard work.
But after a while Friendly listened when I said
"NO," or "SIT," or "STAY." And then I'd say
"GOOD PUPPY" and give her a biscuit.

FETCH!

ROLL OVER!

The bigger Friendly got, the more she learned. Before long, she knew words like "FETCH" and "ROLL OVER." My puppy could do tricks!

Friendly's very favorite word was "PARK."
Whenever I said that, she'd race around and
around in circles with her leash in her mouth.
Then she'd stop and wait for me at the front door.

My puppy is growing up now, but sometimes she still gets into mischief. She still loves Daddy's shoes. And she still loves Mommy's sweaters.
But most of all, she loves ME!